Items should be returned on or before the last date shown below. Items not already requested by other borrowers may be renewed in person, in writing or by telephone. To renew, please quote the number on the barcode label. To renew online a PIN is required. This can be requested at your local library.
Renew online @ **www.dublincitypubliclibraries.ie**
Fines charged for overdue items will include postage incurred in recovery. Damage to or loss of items will be charged to the borrower.

Leabharlanna Poiblí Chathair Bhaile Átha Cliath
Dublin City Public Libraries

Raintree is an imprint of Capstone Global Library Limited, a company incorporated in England and Wales having its registered office at 7 Pilgrim Street, London, EC4V 6LB – Registered company number: 6695582

"Raintree" is a registered trademark of Pearson Education Limited, under licence to Capstone Global Library Limited

Text © Stone Arch Books, 2009
First published by Stone Arch Books in 2008
First published in hardback in the United Kingdom in 2009
First published in paperback in the United Kingdom in 2010
The moral rights of the proprietor have been asserted.

Creative Director: Heather Kindseth
Senior Designer for Cover and Interior: Kay Fraser
Graphic Designer: Brann Garvey
Edited in the UK by Laura Knowles
Printed and bound in China by Leo Paper Products Ltd

ISBN 978-1406212778 (hardback)
13 12 11 10 09
10 9 8 7 6 5 4 3 2 1

ISBN 978-1406212631 (paperback)
14 13 12 11 10
10 9 8 7 6 5 4 3 2 1

British Library Cataloguing in Publication Data
Dahl, Michael.
The twister trap. -- (Library of doom)
813.5'4-dc22
A full catalogue record for this book is available from the British Library.

TABLE OF CONTENTS

The Library of Doom is the world's largest collection of strange and dangerous books. The Librarian's duty is to keep the books from falling into the hands of those who would use them for evil purposes.

❨ CHAPTER 1 ❩

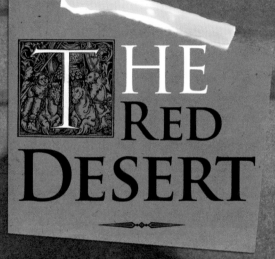

THE RED DESERT

A strange **shadow** passes through a vast, red desert.

The shadow belongs to an **evil magician.** He is known as the Spellbinder.

Under his arms are two strange books, the magical Page Turners.

The books were stolen from the Library of Doom.

When he reaches the middle of the desert, the Spellbinder digs **two holes** in the soft sand.

He lays a book in each hole.

Then he **covers** them with sand.

The Spellbinder chuckles.

A gentle **breeze blows** across the sand.

CHAPTER 2

THE PAGE TURNERS

The wind grows **stronger** and **stronger** and spins above the two buried books.

The breeze turns into **two powerful twisters.**

The Spellbinder **laughs.**

"These Page Turners will bring the Librarian here," he says. "And they will **destroy him!**"

The Librarian has been following
the Spellbinder.

He must find the **stolen** books
and return them to the Library
of Doom.

They are **too powerful** to be
loose in the world.

The Librarian sees two tall twisters in the distance.

He knows these storms are caused by the **Page Turners.**

The Spellbinder must be near.

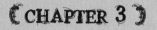

❨ CHAPTER 3 ❩

THE VILLAGE

A few children in a small desert village are playing.

The sky becomes **dark.**

One boy looks up and points.

"A sandstorm!" he shouts.

The **twisters spin** towards
the village.

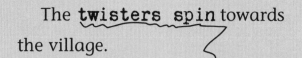

The wind **blows stronger**.
The sky is red, like **blood**.

Sand **whips** through the village.

It stings the villagers' hands
and faces.

As the twisters swirl closer, the
people **run /for shelter.**

The **roof blows** off a building.

It flies towards the **running** boy.

The boy crouches down to hide.

Somewhere, a mother **screams**.

Suddenly, a dark shape `flies out` of the blowing sand.

It is the Librarian.

He pulls the boy to safety. A moment later, the roof **crashes** behind them.

Then the Librarian **leaps** into
one of the swirling twisters.

He must find a way to stop
them.

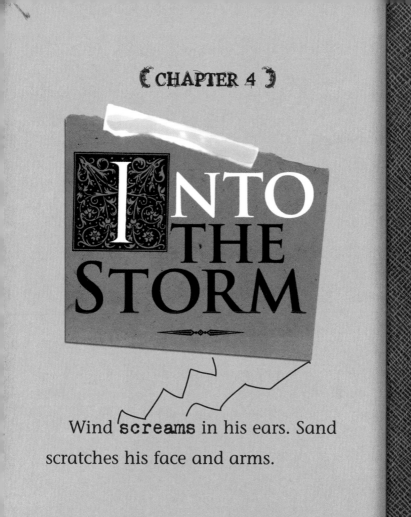

(CHAPTER 4)

INTO THE STORM

Wind **screams** in his ears. Sand scratches his face and arms.

The Librarian cannot fight the powerful, `twisting air.`

The twister pulls the Librarian into its **mighty grip.**

The Librarian cannot see.

He cannot hear anything except the **screaming wind.**

The wind throws the Librarian
through the air as if he were a
broken puppet.

The Librarian **crashes
against** the wall of a house.

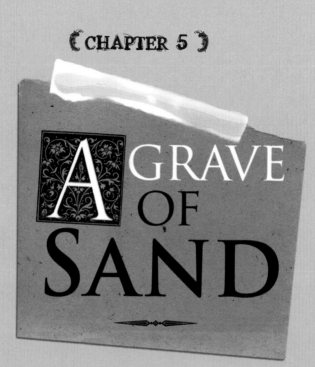

CHAPTER 5

A GRAVE OF SAND

The boy runs to the Librarian.

"Hurry," says the boy. "You can't stay here. The sand will bury you."

The Librarian is **battered** and **bruised**.

He can hardly **hear** the boy.

But he does hear one word.

<u>Bury</u>.

The Librarian crawls to his knees.

He has an **idea.**

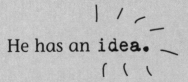

He sees the **twisters** spin 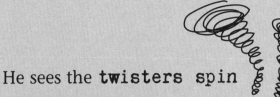 closer to the village.

Then the Librarian begins to **dig**.

He lies down in the **path** of the twisters.

He covers himself with the red sand.

The boy cannot see where the
Librarian went.

All he can see is the twisters as
they burst into the village.

Suddenly, 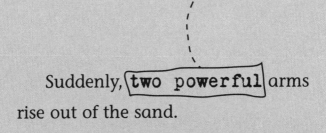 two powerful arms rise out of the sand.

The Librarian holds the two Page Turners in his hands.

The books were moving beneath the sand, guiding the twisters above them.

In the hands of their guardian, the books are now calm.

The winds in the village die
away.

The red sky clears.

The Spellbinder's evil plan has
been defeated.

On a distant desert hill, an
angry shadow turns away.

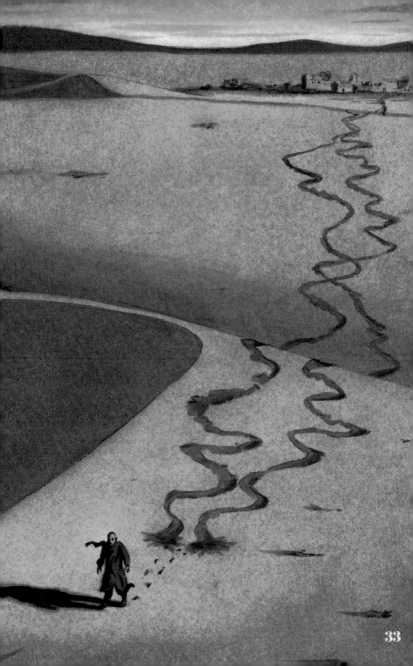

A PAGE FROM THE LIBRARY OF DOOM

MORE ABOUT DESERT STORMS

A sandstorm is caused by strong winds blowing across the surface of a desert or sandy region of Earth.

Sandstorms in Africa's Sahara Desert can blow dust and sand as far away as the United States and Greenland.

Scientists have found desert sand on top of the Alps, Europe's highest mountains. They claim the sand had come from sandstorms.

A Sahara sandstorm is known as a **simoom** (suh-MOOM) or **simoon** (suh-MOON).

Sandstorms are deadly. The rough sand can blow against plants and destroy them. Sand particles can also get in the eyes, noses, and lungs of animals and humans.

A sandstorm known as the **leveche** (luh-VAY-chay) blows red Sahara dust across the sea and into Spain. The winds can reach 100 kpm (60 mph) and last four days!

Ancient legends say that a Persian army of 50,000 soldiers was caught in an Egyptian sandstorm in 521 BCE. The entire army was buried in the sand and the bodies were never found.

ABOUT THE AUTHOR

Michael Dahl is the author of more than 100 books for children and young adults. He has twice won the AEP Distinguished Achievement Award for his non-fiction. His Finnegan Zwake mystery series was chosen by the Agatha Awards to be among the five best mystery books for children in 2002 and 2003. He collects books on poison and graveyards, and lives in a haunted house in Minneapolis, USA.

ABOUT THE ILLUSTRATOR

Bradford Kendall has enjoyed drawing for as long as he can remember. As a boy, he loved to read comic books and watch old monster films. He graduated from the Rhode Island School of Design with a BFA in Illustration. He has owned his own commercial art business since 1983, and lives in Providence, Rhode Island, USA, with his wife, Leigh, and their two children Lily and Stephen. They also have a cat named Hansel and a dog named Gretel.

GLOSSARY

battered (BAT-uhrd) – to be injured by being hit over and over again

chuckle (CHUH-kul) – to laugh quietly

crouches (KROUCH-ez) – gets close to the ground by bending at the knees

defeated (di-FEE-tuhd) – beaten or destroyed by someone else

guardian (GAR-dee-uhn) – someone who protects another person or object

sandstorm (SAND-storm) – strong winds in the desert that blow around lots of sand

twisters (TWISS-turz) – another name for tornadoes, a storm with a violent tunnel of wind that can destroy objects on the ground

vast (VAST) – an extremely large area

village (VIL-ij) – a group of houses or a community that is smaller than a town

DISCUSSION QUESTIONS

1. The Librarian saved the small village and stopped the evil Page Turners. If he could've only done one or the other, what decision would he have made? Explain your answer.

2. At the end of the story, the Spellbinder's plans are defeated. What happened after his plan failed? Do you think he will come after the Librarian again? Why or why not?

3. Illustrations can make a book more exciting. What is your favorite illustration in this book? What did you like about it? How did it make the book more exciting?

WRITING PROMPTS

1. Write a story about your own experience with a storm or bad weather. Was it rain, lightning, thunder, or worse? How did you and your family stay safe?

2. Use your imagination and write more about the Spellbinder character. What is his real name? Where did he grow up? How did he become so evil?

3. The author never reveals what the stories inside the Page Turner books are about. Pretend you are the author of the Page Turners and describe the stories in those books.

MORE BOOKS TO READ

This story may be over, but there are many more dangerous adventures in store for the Librarian. Will the Librarian be able to escape the cave of the deadly giant bookworms? Will he defeat the rampaging Word Eater in time to save the world? You can only find out by reading the other books from the Library of Doom...